MY TEACHER DOESN'T GIVE ME THIS!

Mariam Nalubowa

My Teacher Doesn't Give Me This! / First Edition

ISBN:

978-1-7355344-1-1 (Paperback)

978-1-7355344-0-4 (EBOOK/EPUB)

Dedicated to Michael

Vocabulary

Home-schooled - school at home

Millet - type of grain

Samosa - triangle pastry made with meat or vegetables

Chapati - flatbread

Omelet - beaten eggs cooked in a frying pan

Rolex - chapati with an omelet rolled together

Cultural Day - a day to celebrate different cultures

Once upon a time, many children around the world had to be home-schooled. Kintu was one of them. One morning, his mother called him to sit at the kitchen table to have breakfast before remote learning started.

Excited, he ran to the kitchen but realized that his milk looked brown. "Mama!" he called out. "Someone put dirt in my milk." he complained.

"No my dear, I added warm millet and soy to your milk. In Uganda, that's the type of breakfast children eat." his mother replied. "But my teacher doesn't give me this!" Kintu said. He didn't look happy and didn't want to drink the millet porridge, so she gave him cereal with cold milk.

Kintu enjoyed his math lesson that morning with his mother. He asked his mother to make samosas for lunch.

At lunch time, he was so excited to be called at the kitchen table. He took one bite of the samosa and said, "Mama! I don't like the green stuff you added to my samosa, and it's not spicy."

"My dear, vegetables are healthy, and you don't like spicy food." his mother replied. "But my teacher doesn't give me this!" Kintu said.

At snack time, Kintu walked towards the table very slowly, wondering what his mother had for him. Suddenly, his eyes opened so wide, and he beamed with a smile when he ran across the kitchen to hug her. "You served me cookies with milk. I love you mama. You are the best ever!" he exclaimed. Does your teacher give you this? his mother asked.

No she doesn't, Kintu replied.

At dinner time, the aroma from the kitchen made him feel so hungry. His mother had made a chapati, which is a flat bread, and then turned it into a rolex by spreading an omelet on it and adding lettuce plus raw tomatoes and then folding it like a wrap.

"Kintu, dinner is ready." his mother called out. He rushed to the table and sat down with a big smile. He looked at his plate and asked his mother what that was. She told him that in Uganda, it's called a rolex, and she explained to him how it's prepared.

"Is this healthy?" he asked. "Yes my dear, it's very healthy and tasty." his mother replied.

He ate his dinner quietly.

"Mama, my teacher doesn't give me this, but I really enjoyed it and would like to present this for cultural day at my school." Kintu said. "Of course dear, and tomorrow we shall prepare one together with a sprinkle of cheese." his mother said as she hugged him tight.

Fun questions to share with your child

1. How does Kintu feel about dinner?

2. Where did the story happen?

3. What African country is mentioned in the story?

4. Who was the main character in the story?

5. Does Kintu like home schooling?

Have your child draw a picture of their homeschool experience.

Fun family activity: make a samosa

Ingredients

1 packet pastry wraps (10 pieces)

1 lb ground turkey, beef or chicken

1 onion

1/3 cup cilantro

1 tsp salt

1 egg

Cooking oil

<u>Preparation</u>

Chop and add onions, cilantro, salt and ground turkey into pan and stir until cooked and all the water has dried out. Then let it cool off completely.

Defrost pastry wraps

Beat the egg. Fold the wrap into a triangle leaving one side open and add the cooked ground turkey using a spoon and make sure not to overfill. With your finger tips use the beaten egg by rubbing some of it at the opening of your triangle to seal it. Continue with all until done.

Heat up the oil in a frying pan and place the triangles in. Turn them over when brown, remove from pan. Serve hot or cold with desired sauce or beverage.

THE END

www.ingramcontent.com/pod-product-compliance
Lightning Source LLC
Chambersburg PA
CBHW081359090726
47908CB00011B/2734